ISIS: A Love Story

Abu Salaam

© 2016

*To Syria*

1

Blazing down the desert road, the truck tore a cloud of sun-scorched dust in its wake.

Under the duct tape, the driver's hands dripped with sweat against the worn vinyl steering wheel. He barreled closer to his destination. Closer.

Closer.

It was in sight now, only a few hundred meters away. Its rigid geometric form contrasted the surrounding slopes of sand.

His time had come. This was his moment. He inhaled one last, then:

"Allahu Akbar!"

The truck punched into the wall of the airbase, detonating immediately upon impact, rumbling the foundation, and screaming its battle cry through the hot summer air, a flaming hole of rubble the only proof of its existence.

Just seconds later and meters away, the second truck reached its destination. Then the third. The drivers yelled their Takbir graces to Allah then pummeled the structure with a succession of blasts.

Next came the pickup trucks and SUVs. Toyotas, a whole convoy of dozens. Ali and Majnun were in the 11th, same as last time. It was their lucky one. They hadn't become martyrs yet.

Majnun gripped tightly to his Kalashnikov as he rushed to mutter one last prayer. His bent knee, pressed against Ali's, providing the only comfort in the tense moment. Ali reached out and patted his thigh:

"Brother relax! We've got this! You've got me and I've got you!"

Majnun looked up to meet Ali's gaze. Their eyes briefly locked. He nodded.

#11 jostled forward, bouncing over the wreckage created by the third truck.

They flew a few hundred meters more and screeched to a halt in front of a row of plain barracks buildings.

As soon as the vehicle stopped, the occupants chambered rounds into their rifles and swung the doors open in unison. The gunfire was heavy here. Loud cracks and sulfurous odor permeated from every direction, compounding density to the thick air.

Ali and Majnun circled the back of the SUV to meet at the rear bumper. Together they surveyed the situation, scouting for cover that would protect them against a counter-assault from Government troops.

"There!" yelled Majnun, his voice lost to the din of the environment. He pointed to a wall of sand bags that lined the back of the barracks buildings.

It was surrounded on three sides and capable of taking small arms fire - the perfect cover.

A hand to Majnun's back showed Ali's only affirmative response. They sprinted towards it.

Reaching the barricade, they stopped and nuzzled down close to its protection. Taking a few seconds to catch their breath, they prepared for the onslaught that lie on the other side.

In unison, they counted down on their fingers. Three. Two. One.

They popped up and immediately began spraying cover fire in the general direction of their enemy. Majnun shot left and Ali shot right. Before them was a scene of chaos. Burnt out trucks littered the vast air strip. Masked fighters at one end traded sustained fire with uniformed Government troops at the other.

The smell of gunfire was now met with the smell of burning diesel fuel and the smell of death.

Ali's magazine emptied first. With a shout of: "Reload!" He ducked behind the wall.

A few seconds later, Majnun followed with: "Me too!"

With their backs to the sand bags, they levered out the empty mags and tossed them onto the hot spent shell casings at their feet. Replacing them with fresh from their pouches, they racked the bolts of their AKs and sprang up. Now with specific targets to hone into, they started spraying fire anew.

Their continued assault drew the attention of a garrison of defense troops who started spraying the sandbag wall with lead.

Ali and Majnun pelted return counter-fire until the stream of bullets from their rifles ceased. Pressing down against the wall, they reloaded again.

The cacophony of their clash rang through the air. Meeting each other's eyes, they counted down again with their fingers. At zero, they sprang in unison, spraying steady fire at the garrison targeting them. Their aim was true and their shots sure - successfully downing a number of Loyalist troops.

Ducking back to catch their breath, they turned to each other with smiles. They shared no words. Expressions alone carried the conversation.

Perceiving no further fire, they rose to their feet, ears still ringing from the continued assault.

Finally, Ali celebrated their success by yelling to Majnun: "Not martyrs yet!"

Majnun couldn't hear the words but still he understood perfectly.

As he read Ali's lips, a gun barrel rose downrange.

He saw the flashes before he heard them.

Then felt them. Tearing through the top sand bag, hot chunks of lead sprayed sand in all directions. It stung Majnun's lips, yet he didn't shield them. Nor did he rush to return fire. Instead, instinctively, he dive tackled Ali.

Hands wrapped around Ali's skinny jeans, Majnun tried his best to prevent a hard impact. Bringing his own body to the ground first, he rolled Ali's on top of it.

They lay there for a moment. Stunned. Shocked. Exhilarated. Face-to-face. Sand and bullets sprayed over their joined bodies. Still they stayed unharmed.

Realizing this, the Mujahiduo elated. Ali's joy sprang forth as a kiss onto Majnun's lips. He lingered for a moment, enjoying the life in his companion. Then, rolling his body off, Ali rocked a full magazine into his rifle. Under pressure, he rose- spraying fire at his foe. Adrenaline and amphetamine steadied his muscles.

With perfect aim, his shots flowed through to their target - lighting up the soldier and dropping him flat.

Relieved of opposition, Ali and Majnun took a restful moment to collect themselves.

Tossing their hot-barreled rifles gently into the shade, they began refilling their empty magazines from the bandoliers across their chests.

Majnun started: "I thought I lost you for a second, that you were hit."

Ali smiled graciously: "I might have been if not for you brother. I have your back and I'm lucky you have mine."

Saying this, he ran a steady hand down Majnun's back for effect.

Majnun smiled reluctantly, set down the mag he was loading, and reciprocated the gesture.

The firefight had drained them. As the battle for the airbase continued around them, they took a necessary moment to take comfort in each other. It was the only comfort they had in the shelled out landscape, but it was enough.

2

The punctuating cracks of gunfire eased as their periodicity lost proportion to the strange silence.

Finally, the shots stopped all together as the last clashes were won.

Soon after the fighting ceased, Mustafa Azazi, Regional Commander at Tabqa, bounced up in his Toyota pickup. His hand slammed jubilantly on the horn- a sign for the fighters to come near.

Ali and Majnun steadied their rifles on their backs and trotted to join the semi-circle of muharibūn already gathered around the vehicle's ecstatic occupant.

"Congratulations lions! By the grace of Allah, we have seized this fortress from the forces of hell-dogs loyal to Bashar Al-Assad!"

He spat on the ground for good measure.

"In one hour we will march the remaining kuffar cowards outside the perimeter of our new home. There they will be extinguished. Then, the rest of the day is yours to rest and pray. You have earned this lions-Savor it."

The eyes of several of the fighters lit up in anticipation of gore and death. They launched into hoots and holler of "Allahu Akbar" and began blasting bullets into the air.

Ali and Majnun examined each other nervously- this wasn't the jihad they'd enlisted for. Killing a man on the battlefield was a necessary part of the struggle. But this? Labeling captured brothers as kuffar and massacring them? It was Takfir- the worst kind of haraam.

Still they retained their silence. Questioning a superior officer's mandate was akin to treason, doing so would get them labeled traitors of the State- they'd be forced into martyrdom. Or shot on sight.

Their next hour was spent outside of the barracks they'd helped claim. Irritable from the comedown of the Captagon high they rode during the battle, and anxious at the task ahead, they spoke little. Instead, they used the time to rehydrate their bodies and silently swab the barrels of their assault rifles.

Seeing their comrades gather the mass of humanity to the center of the base, Ali and Majnun knew it was time to go.

Arriving to the congregate mass, they joined the perimeter of mujahideen encircling the men.

Under threats of death, the Loyalist soldiers were forced to strip to their underwear and form a double-file column.

Many of the mujahideen took the opportunity to yell curses and taunts at their powerless enemy.

Absent the zeal of their compatriots, Majnun and Ali followed behind the desperate group with their sidearms silently raised.

Two kilometers outside of the airbase perimeter, a backhoe idled next to a significant mound of fresh earth. Seeing this, the faces of the captives rendered quickly from the mere shame of a defeat to total shock and despair.

One of the Loyalist troops broke from the column to plead for mercy from his captors: "Please! We are brothers in Allah! It is Takfir to bring harm to a believer!"

Commander Azazi shot the man twice in the stomach:

"I am not brothers with a dog."

Turning to the operator of the backhoe, Commander Azazi roared:

"Deeper! I don't want to smell their death from my new home!"

The fighters, thrilled again with the prospect of death en masse, erupted into more gunfire and Takbir exclamations.

As the backhoe dug, Commander Azazi ordered the men at the front of the column to advance. A waiting bulldozer rumbled on into neutral in anticipation of the event. Commander Azazi halted the front of the column directly in front of it.

Turning to his pride of lions, he smiled:

"Target practice."

Leading by example, he drew his pistol and began firing at the group of men.

Blood splattered and a number of the mujahideen joined in- emptying their clips into the half-clothed cluster of humanity.

The dead piled up into a bloody blob. Commander Azazi order the dozer to advance- then ordered more of the column to step forward onto the now blood-soaked ground.

This cycle continued for too long.

At no point did Majnun or Ali participate in the slaughter. The bloodlust of their comrades forbade the necessity.

When the dozer made its final sweep, a thick red mat replaced what had hours before been arid ground. Track marks through it told the toll that had been taken.

Mujahideen exploded into shouts of Takbir, eyes wide with madness and amphetamines.

Ali vomited. Majnun offered water in an attempt to blame the heat for the sudden nausea. Ali loudly accepted.

Commander Azazi again congratulated his lions and with a prayer, dismissed them for the day.

Although offered a ride back to base, Ali declined. He preferred instead to walk the sandy road with Majnun.

It was fully dark by the time they re-breached the perimeter. The remote airbase offered spacious views of the stars, but neither Majnun nor Ali lingered to enjoy them. After the day's events, both desired only sleep.

That night they found it in one of the empty barracks buildings they'd helped conquer.

3

It was morning. The cool in the air was already giving way to the heat of the day. Ali struggled to decipher the map he'd printed for his trip.

The streets were strange and he was sweating. Panning his eyes nervously, he searched for a familiar face but found none. Frustrated, he looked back to his map for guidance, but found it still absent.

At the point of exasperation, a familiar and comforting voice spoke from behind him:

"Salaam alaikum brother, maybe we can walk together."

Everything was so real. So vivid.

Spinning 180° - Ali was met face-to-face with the warmth of Majnun's fiery brown eyes.

"Walaikum Assalaam brother, I am lost."

Ali breathed the words directly to Majnun's lips.

Majnun aspirated his response in return:

"Then I will show you the way."

Majnun laced his fingers into his companion's and began stride.

Immersed in clarity, Ali found the haze surrounding him vanquished-both mentally and physically.

Soon after, they arrived at the Internet cafe. The path to it seemed so obvious in hindsight. Inside was the fixer that would take them into Syria.

He shook, then kissed their hands - the signal that it was he for whom they searched.

He gave his speech explaining that he would take them to a safe-house apartment to wait for nightfall.

Leading them out of the cafe, he signaled to a dirty white sedan parked on the street.

Kilis was suddenly full of people and vehicles. It was a normal sunny summer day.

As their driver gained speed, winds started to whirl and lightning split the skies. The happy people milling about their daily lives started to panic. Fear became evident in their faces.

As the thunder came into range, explosions started. Cars all around them began to pop off. Their loud blasts quickly became indistinguishable from thunder in the chaos.

Strength and frequency of the blasts increased. They were so many, and so close, that Majnun and Ali could feel the shockwaves pulse through their bodies.

Still they remained unharmed.

They were the storm.

They sped into the desert. The frenzied Turkish civilians had vanished. In their stead roamed thousands of half-naked Syrian Loyalist troops. Bloody bullet holes dotted their bodies and hollow bored through their eyes.

The fixer's beater car had transformed without either of them realizing it. It was now #11- in its latest incarnation- a Toyota SUV.

Now with room to stretch, both remained huddled down as if still in the beater.

The Toyota's head lights shone as the sole source of luminosity into the darkness of the desert.

Road signs showed that their route led to Raqqa.

Slaughtered Syrian soldiers roamed the desert to infinity. Their bodies moved, but their blank eyes stayed fixed on the Toyota.

Terrified by their surroundings, Ali and Majnun sought comfort in each other. Running hands over each other's warm bodies, the terror from around the ceased. The car sped on and the bodies swarmed but it didn't matter.

All that mattered is that they were together. Their hands wandered and their lips found each other's. Desire swirled in their minds.

4

Majnun awoke with sleepy eyes and the confusion that comes with waking in a bed that is not your own. Tracing a hand over the crotch in his skinny jeans, he was relieved to find that the bulge in them remained occluded.

Ali lie behind him, still asleep but similarly afflicted. His peaceful repose accented only by indiscernible slumber-speak.

Rising to his feet, Majnun fell quickly into remembrance of the dream. What did it mean? Why did he have it?

Maybe it was a trick- born from chemical concoctions composed by the Americans. Or even the Jews.

He quickly exorcised the thought from his mind. Even with their technical abilities, they couldn't possibly produce something so pure. So real.

Exiting the barracks, he paused to bask and contemplate in the warm morning sun.

Maybe it was a trial from Allah - a test.

Surely Allah could create something so pure. But why would he test his faithful servant?

Caught in the thought, Majnun didn't notice the Dawlah tagged SUV driving towards him until it was mere meters away.

The driver exited, and, after a quick exchange of "Salaams", informed Majnun that Commander Azazi required his presence in the Operations Building.

Majnun thanked the man and turned to open the barracks door, to inform Ali of his destination. The man's hand on his shoulder stopped him mid-movement: "Commander Azazi requires your presence right now."

Majnun returned to the barracks on foot. His eyes carried the appearance that they had recently carried tears. This was immediately evident to Ali, who drew a look of concern.

"Brother you've been crying-" He strode to Majnun's side.

"-What's wrong?"

Majnun wavered: "Tabqa will not be our home for long. Tonight we join a convoy for Kobane."

Ali's concern intensified. Kobane front was known for claiming the highest number of martyrs lost in battle.

"Why?"

"Azazi did not say. Only that we would go." The tears that Majnun had worked to clear from his eyes again sprang forth.

Ali's arms brought their bodies together. Majnun's head fell to Ali's shoulders, grateful for the embrace. His tears flowed freely.

Ali searched for the words that would make them stop: "Wherever we go, we will go together. You have me and I you."
Majnun dried his eyes on Ali's shirt and raised them to meet Ali's: "You have me and I you."

The following few hours were spent somber, far from the celebrations they'd anticipated after such a large battle gain.

Was their incidental encounter on the battlefield witnessed?

Or was it their lack of zeal in participating in the massacre?

Did Azazi arrange to send them to Kobane to make them into martyrs, or because he believed they were capable of avoiding such a fate?

At the prescribed time, purged of emotionality, Ali and Majnun arrived at the operations building. A small line of vehicles wait parked outside. Mujahideen milled about, awaiting a final clearance from Commander Azazi. None looked as anxious as Ali and Majnun felt.

Finally, the beast of a man burst forth from the doorway:

"Lions, you have displayed your prowess here at Tabqa Airbase-" he waved his arms at their surroundings. "-Now it is time for you to display the power of the Dawlah in Kobane."

Some of the fighters lit up, ignorant of the number of Kobane casualties, or excited by it.

Azazi continued: "In death Allah offers you 72 virgins, but in life I can offer you only this one-"

On cue, a line of shackled Yazidi girls were led from the Operations Room at gunpoint.

"For your valiant efforts."

At the sight, the stale desires of the mujahideen flared- the lust in their eyes met the fear in the Yazidis.

One-by-one, the girls were unlocked and placed with mujahid.

Azazi unleashed a brief ceremony: speaking the words, he said, that would lawfully bind them in the eyes of Allah.

Now bound, Majnun and Ali took stock of their wives.

5

The convoy traveled through the night, lit several times by only the light of the moon, as the drivers sought to avoid scrutiny from Government planes.

As the sun's rays reached over the horizon, signs for Kobane became visible along the roadside.

As they grew near, the column of vehicles splintered- taking route to the destinations assigned by Azazi.

Soon, the only vehicles remaining were the two carrying Majnun and Ali.

Separately, they grew restless - increasingly convinced that their reassignment was merely a ploy to execute them away from the other mujahideen.

Fear in their eyes mirrored that of their wives. They fought to suppress it. Using the thought of each other to fight the fear, they regained composure just as their transport arrived at a police station flying the black flag.

Coming to a full stop, Ali's driver entered the building while Majnun's waited outside with the fighters and their wives. Moments later, the driver returned, followed closely by a gray-bearded man in a Ba'ath officer's uniform.

The man thanked the drivers and then waved them off, leaving the man alone with Majnun, Ali, and their wives.

"Assalamu alaikum lions. Welcome to Kobane."

Ali and Majnun replied with nervous "Salaams" as their fear of immediate execution replaced with an uncertain prospect of martyrdom missions.

"I am Abu Shami, regional commander of Kobane district. Congratulations on your recent success at Tabqa and thank you for joining me."

Ali and Majnun exchanged glances, skeptical of the pleasantry that arrived only as a result of their lack of choice.

"Commander Azazi has sent word of your battle accomplishments and has implored me to find you a place on the front-lines."

Tears welled in Ali's eyes and Majnun forced a hard swallow.

Abu Shami continued:

"I myself however, believe in rewarding achievements with rest. As such, for the next few weeks, you will be positioned at a checkpoint

Southeast of the city. It opens to state-held territory, and should be absent the action you've seen recently at Tabqa."

With a genuine smile, the man finished:

"Assuming you're alright with relinquishing a little excitement."

Relieved, Majnun and Ali smiled back, assuring the man they had no problem doing so.

"Good. It is encouraging to see such young men take up the jihad. I think you will find Kobane very suitable."

Ali and Majnun charged their phones in the police station as they stacked bottled water and canisters of ammo into the bed of a State-marked pickup.

With only two seats in the cab, their wives had to ride in the bed with the water and ammunition. The girls, whose stress levels had already hit peak, were simply largely indifferent to the atypical travel arrangement.

Abu Shami gave them a map and a sendoff and they pressed to the Southeast.

Their drive to the checkpoint, though only a few dozen kilometers in distance, lasted more than three hours. Owing to the duration were a minefield and two other State-held checkpoints. Referred to as "friendly" checkpoints, most mujahideen knew this was rarely the case.

After waiting a tense hour in a vehicle queue at each, and providing their travel writs and identification documents to four sets of guards, they were cleared through to the open highway to the checkpoint they'd be working.

They arrived just before sundown. Only one guard was awake to accept their documents. The only other guard at the outpost snored in a construct-shanty a few meters away.

Reading Majnun and Ali's travel writs, the already animate guard moved with excitement to awaken his sleeping companion and announce their arrival.

The wildly bearded man shot up, eyes wild to match. Instinctively, he grabbed for his rifle.

Ali and Majnun jumped back, startled. From the pickup bed, their wives cringed.

Analyzing and reassessing the situation with sleepy eyes, the man realized there was no immediate threat. With a sleepy "Salaam

Alaikum", he set back contentedly on his chair.

His more awake counterpart smiled off the occurrence:

"Sleep is premium priced in these parts. Inshallah, with you here, that will change."

Through forced smiles, Majnun and Ali nodded in unison: "Inshallah."

"Your training shift starts tomorrow at 6:00AM. Until then, feel free to rest and relax in some of the fine accommodations this part of Kobane has to offer."

With the words, the man raised his rifle and pointed it at a subdivision of tightly packed houses a few hundred meters away.

With a set of farewell "Salaams", Majnun and Ali stepped back into their pickup and Ali peeled down the pavement toward their new home.

6

The sun's colors, spilling over the horizon, gave way to darkness as they reached the subdivision.

Small houses lined empty streets. Choosing one, Ali and Majnun led the girls inside.

The interior was already dark but with the light from their cell phones they were able to get comfortably situated.

The home looked like it was rapidly abandoned. Lanterns dotted through the rooms showed it was likely after electricity had been cut to the area.

Majnun lit two. Handing one to the girls, he kept the other for himself.

Fear in the girls' eyes showed that they would not venture out into the night alone. Content with that knowledge, Majnun and Ali left them at the house and went out to explore the neighborhood.

The streets were nearly dark but the gas-light from the lantern cast a warm hue as they walked. Majnun held it to his side, and their fingers met between them, shrouded in darkness.

One house with an attached garage looked particularly inviting. Ali and Majnun examined it together. Lifting on the garage door in unison, they found it unlocked.

Inside, a car nested in the garage, surrounded by boxes of belongings overfilled from the house.

Lifting the flaps on one, Ali found a box of dolls and books. Looking down at it, he turned to Majnun:

"Do you think it is still haraam to take things that have been abandoned?"

Majnun breathed in with thought before replying:

"I think whoever left this here wasn't planning on coming back for it.

Ali nodded, content with the answer:

"I think I'm going to take this back for the girls."

Majnun smiled at Ali's sincerity:

"I think they would like it."

Checking the other boxes, they found nothing more than blankets and glassware. So they continued inside.

The living room layout was reminiscent of the house they'd left the girls at.

A door from the living room led directly to a girl's bedroom-distinctive immediately because of its bright colors.

Ali looked contemplatively at the contents: "Do you think they got out alive?"

"I hope so."

"Me too."

Ali added a few more books to the box and then moved onward.

Ahead, a hallway branched off. Ali went up to the master bedroom and Majnun went down to find the kitchen.

"Hey come look!" Ali called from the back bedroom.

Majnun darted up the few steps from the kitchen, piercing the doorway with a handful of chocolate bars.

"For the girls" he explained, tucking them into the box of dolls and books.

"Look!" exclaimed Ali, shining his phone's flashlight to an open dresser drawer. Stacked inside were a collection of American produced porn magazines, now considered contraband in the Caliphate.

Majnun picked up a Penthouse and Ali grabbed a Hustler. Flipping through the pages, they pointed out the most graphic pictures they could find- trying to outdo each other's level of explicitness.

Majnun motioned to one money-shot and Ali reactively rubbed his longing loins.

"I would love such sweet release."

"So then let's not miss the opportunity."

Majnun unfastened his belt and undid his pants and Ali quickly followed.

In the dim light of the lantern, they stripped off their shirts and underwear, standing fully naked in each other's light.

Their interest in the magazines diminished and they drew involuntarily together. Weak attempts to resist were abandoned as the fighters quickly capitulated their desires to each other.

They stood, transfixed on each other's growing arousal, standing over the stranger's bed.

Ali raised his eyes to be level with Majnun's. Sensing this, Majnun looked up. Their eyes locked and they gazed intently into each other. They could see what each other desired. Majnun reached over to extinguish the lantern.

In the darkness, their hands traced over each other's battle-toned bodies. Ali pressed a gentle guiding hand to Majnun's bare body, nudging him toward the bed. They climbed up and lied down side-by-side next to each other. Their hands reached across each other and their lips met. They tasted and felt each other with increasing passion, growing near frenzy as they neared release.

They found release together. Their mouths froze together mid-movement and their hands pulsed on each other, trying to prolong the moment of shared ecstasy. The bliss blurred their bodies and minds together. Slowly, Ali and Majnun's unpinned arousal faded to a mildly awkward contentment. The muharibūn, still pressed together, quietly contemplated what had just happened.

Finally, Ali spoke:

"At least stationed here we can get a shower."

He rose, ducking into the adjacent bathroom. Majnun heard the water start to flow and followed him.

The tiny bathroom was lit only by the reflected luminosity of the moon shining through the doorway, and the water was cold. Still, under it, Majnun and Ali found light and warmth in each other. With their hands, they wiped clean the weeks of tension spilled across each other. Then, reaching around, they folded into each other's warm embrace under the cool flow.

Ali and Majnun left the house as the colors on the horizon hinted that the sun was again growing near.

Stopping by the main house, they dropped off the books and toys and chocolates. They also left instructions:

"We will return to the house at least once a day, to check on you. If we are ever gone for more than a full day, open the front door of the house, gather your belongings, and lock yourself in the bathroom."

This, explained Ali, would show that the house was abandoned and not worth searching further.

Majnun jumped in to show the girls a special code knock, so they would know exactly who was on the other side of the door.

The girls didn't ask why they were being spared the savageries inflicted on some of the other girls. Nor did they ask why their husbands both returned with wet heads. They were too young to possess more than a rudimentary understanding of why their husbands brought them gifts and left them untouched, but they were appreciative nonetheless.

7

They arrived at 6:04 AM according to Ali's cell phone. Majnun's was still dead. Several attempts to connect it to the charger at just the right angle had failed.

The two guards at the checkpoint were both awake- looking like they'd barely slept.

Tired bags hung under large pupils but still they greeted Majnun and Ali with welcome graces.

It was a nice change of pace, being treated like equals again.

The first guard formally introduced himself as Hamdi, and the wildly bearded man introduced himself as Omar.

Starting with the important business, Hamdi pulled an ammo pouch from his backpack.

"I've got something for you."

Unfastening it, he pulled out two full blister packs of pills and tossed one to both Majnun and Ali.

Pulling out a third, half-punched pack, he popped two pills from their foil before explaining:

"Here closer to the border with Turkey-" He motioned to a direction

that may or may not have been
accurate.

"-These are easier to procure
than where you come from in Raqqa."

Ali clarified: "Thank you for
your gift but we come from Tabqa."

Omar stroked his beard and
Hamdi's eyes lit up further:

"Yes Tabqa! Very impressive!
They are definitely easier to
procure here than Tabqa!"

He laughed.

Ali and Majnun smiled along.
Not wanting to appear under-
appreciative, they both punched out
and dry swallowed a Captagon tablet.

Omar and Hamdi smiled. Hamdi
slit two bottles from a pack stacked
in the bed of the pickup and tossed
one to mujahideen.

Ali and Majnun took
appreciative sips, then assisted
Hamdi as he began unloading the rest
of the supplies they'd brought.

Omar slipped into the lean-to
outpost and came out with a placard
board lined with phone chargers. He
tossed one to Majnun:

"I saw you were having some
trouble- is this the right fit?"

Majnun checked the tip:

"Yeah looks like a match.
Shukran."

Omar nodded his approval:

"Confiscated from enemy forces."

Majnun's smile faded -though grateful for the gift- he doubted the genuineness of its origin.

Hamdi set down the last of the ammunition then turned to Majnun and Ali with a more serious face than they'd seen:

"Working rural checkpoints is easy business. I think you will like it. I suspect you already do. Less work and less people however means less chance of help arriving if something goes wrong. There may be no backup, remember that when making your decisions."

The serious speech was met with solemn nods from Ali and Majnun.

Contented with their understanding, Hamdi lightened. Tussling Majnun's hair, he looked at Ali's:

"Why is your hair so wet? Get caught in a storm?"

Caught off guard, Majnun fabricated:

"We spent our first night in town enjoying time in our new houses with our new wives. We wanted to purify our bodies in the ways prescribed by the Prophet, peace be upon him."

Ali nodded.

Hamdi smiled slyly:

"How was your first night?"

Ali met Majnun's glance with a quick grin:

"Even better than expected."

Hamdi trumped strong hands on the backs of both mujahideen. "Congratulations lions."

Over the next few easy hours, Omar and Hamdi taught Majnun and Ali the logistics behind running a rural checkpoint: how to read travel writs, find contraband, and keep the queue organized. Between cars, the men recounted their top conquests. Ali and Majnun excitedly orated the tale of the Battle of Tabqa Airbase while Omar and Hamdi listened with intrigue.

One SUV pulled up and beeped its horn, like the others. Two men occupied it.

"Papers please."

One of the men stammered that he didn't have papers then launched into a clumsy explanation of why.

Hamdi cut the man off with an open hand:

"No problem, we'll just have to search the vehicle. Pop the trunk and hood please."

The men complied and Hamdi moved to the front of the vehicle while Omar circled to the back.

Opening the hood, Hamdi crouched down behind the engine block. Omar lifted the trunk.

From the lean-to Majnun and Ali looked with curiosity. Then-

Omar drew his sidearm and cocked it back. In seconds the entire mag emptied into the cab of the vehicle.

He popped the mag, hit the slide release, loaded a fresh magazine, and re-holstered his side arm.

Hamdi rose and slammed the hood of the vehicle. Omar did the same to the now bullet-ridden trunk.

Ali and Majnun looked shocked from the lean-to.

"What the hell are you doing!? You shot two innocent men!"

"Listen-" said Hamdi with the sternest expression they'd seen. "Two men without papers is a very dangerous situation."

Omar cut in to continue:

"Just last week we had two Nusra recruits hit the checkpoint."

Hamdi nodded his agreement.

Uncertain, Ali and Majnun turned to refind their certainty in each other.

The remainder of their shift passed tersely. At just after 6:00 PM, Omar and Hamdi congratulated the pair on becoming professionally trained State checkpoint guards.

Free for the day, Ali and Majnun retreated to the house with the girls for rest before their 6:00 AM solo shift.

8

It was raining.

Strangest here of all places. A training camp in the Syrian desert; the place that had cultivated the state into what it now was.

It dropped on the vinyl roof of the tent barracks like sprinkled salt, speaking softly.

Ali rolled over to his left and found exactly what he expected to: Majnun lying on the cot next to his. He too was wearing only his underwear.

Kilis was where they first met but this is where they first really bonded. The two weeks of hell had promised to transform new recruits from weak cubs to strong lions. When Majnun cried, it was Ali who comforted him. It was here that they made a pact, to always have each other's backs. They rose, embraced, kissed, and laced fingers. Hand-in-hand they led each other down the row of cots, through the door flaps.

The training grounds and target range were saturated. A thick dark cloud dripped its contents over all. The sight, though bleak, bore a strange beauty.

Wonderfilled, something compelled them up and over the rocky outcropping, a place they'd never before ventured.

As they ascended, the rocks grew. Still they scaled them, helping each other each step of the way.

Racing higher, they pushed to outpace the growth, until finally, through the torrent, Majnun managed his fingertips over the final ledge.

He struggled.

Held by only his right foot and fingertips, he held his body to the rock wall.

Sweeping with his left foot, he searched for the ledge that could boost him to safety.

Finding none, he became certain he would fall. His strength wouldn't last. He accepted his near doom and waited for his muscles to fade from fatigue.

He hoped only that Ali would make it out alive.

Then, a boost from below.

Ali, gripping the facade with only his feet, laced his fingers into an artificial ledge. Finding this footing, Majnun maneuvered up and over the edge.

Exhausted but relieved, he rolled onto his stomach and reached a hand back down for Ali:

"You had me, now I have you."

Ali pulled himself over the precipice and on top of Majnun.

"I still have you."

The storms started to subside to sprinkles, thinning into spots of sunshowers.

Ali moved his lips to the back of Majnun's neck and left them there motionless.

More sun shined through, arcing a rainbow across the sky. It spilled its colors to the grounds below.

Beauty shined over brutality.

They watched it warmly together until curiosity again compelled them- to see where the other end had fallen.

With surprise, they discovered that the other side of the rocky outcropping fell not to sharp cliffs but sloped to lush green and flowers.

The rainbow dashed its colors overhead and sprayed them onto the suburb below.

Hand-in-hand, they descended.

Though their sole coverings
were soaked translucent with water,
they walked without shame.

Colors in the sky and fields
provided welcome relief from the
tired tan of the desert.


The first house they came to
had a vehicle parked outside. It was
refit with seats, and its State
insignia replaced with a fresh wax
job. Still it was without a doubt,
#11.

Majnun cupped his hands to peer
through the back windows. Ali to the
front.

Trying a door, Ali found it
unlocked. On the passenger seat
rested two Ak-47s, Majnun's and his
own.

Picking up both by their
handguards, he passed one to Majnun.

Majnun set it down, leaning
against the vehicle, distracted by
something in the backseat.

Opening the door, he pulled out
a child carrier seat. His eyes and
Ali's transfixed on it, then each
other's.

Suddenly, the extraordinary
sight was eclipsed by something more
so.

On the ground, Majnun's weapon had taken root. It sprouted shoots and grew upwards.

Instinctively, Ali unslung his own rifle and propped it next to Majnun's.

It too sprung up, growing thick and skyward.

Together they rose and intertwined, growing strong and bearing fruit.

Olives draped in abundance from their branches, still they did not bend.


Continuing into the house, Ali and Majnun found themselves suddenly wrapped in robes of black flags.

The interior of the house they recognized as one from a house in Kobane.

The belongings inside they had never before seen. Still, they knew they were not the possessions of strangers, but their own.

Expansive bedrooms defied the limits of the house. Inside were a brood of beautiful children. Features from both of them shared on their faces. In them though, Ali saw only Majnun and Majnun only Ali.

Through this light they suddenly became embarrassed by the

darkness that draped them, regretful to taint the light.

But the children cast no judgment in their eyes.

They stayed there together as a family and time passed.

They were happy.

More happy and for longer than they ever had been.

The trees and their love grew.

They were happy.

9

The next several days passed blissfully uneventfully for Ali and Majnun.

Working the checkpoint was easy duty. No situation had required the brutal maneuvers they'd been taught. 12 hours on and 12 hours off allowed them time to themselves, away from the base of the state.

They stopped in to see the girls each day with gifts of books and toys and candy. The girls enjoyed the gifts and Majnun and Ali enjoyed being able to provide them. With the gifts, they left the same instructions and code knock, before going out to explore the abandoned neighborhood.

In the shelled-out homes of the area, they found time for numerous other small encounters.

As their passions inflated, time spent off-duty became insufficient to meet their growing desires, trysts spilled over into their checkpoint duty.

At maximum only a few cars per hour needed cleared. It was Ramadan, the heat and holiness of the days opted people away from traveling. Those that did could be waved through without hesitation.

Ali and Majnun lie content with the knowledge that the other two mujahideen who manned the outpost would not return until required.

During the days it pushed over 40C. The lean-to hut provided relief from the suns light but not its heat. Under it, Majnun fixed a tarp to the open side, obscuring nearly all of the interior from view of the queue.

In the new found privacy they stripped down together, allowing sweat to purge heat from their bodies.

Together they lounged in their underwear, thankful for both the reprieve from the heat and the time alone together.

A car beeped its horn outside and Ali rose, peeling the tarp flap just enough to reveal his face.

"Salaam Alaikum. Papers please."

A nervous looking family answered with "Salaams" as they shuffled through a thin stack of documents.

From his seat, Majnun eyed up Ali's standing form. Its faint shimmer of sweat glistened invitingly.

A car door opened and closed and Ali reached his hand out to accept the papers from the family's father. A cursory check found them in order, so with a "Salaam" he returned the papers and waved the family through.

Scouting his seat, Ali started to return to it- but Majnun countered:

"No. Stay up."

Ali obeyed.

On his knees, Majnun crawled to Ali. With his hands, he slid across the slick coating on Ali's toned legs and with his mouth he tasted it from Ali's tanned abs. He savored its sweet salinity.

Majnun's lips moved further south, brushing kisses over the trimmed hair. He continued down the length of Ali's growing tower, meeting eyes with Ali as he did. Taking Ali in his mouth, Majnun moved rhythmically. Ali let out a small moan and pressed his hands to the back of Majnun's head.

"Salaam lions!-"

With the quick announcement, Omar walked in to the exposed end of the lean-to. He picked up the pouch he came for, then looked at Majnun and Ali- now separate but still in compromising positions.

Piecing together what he was seeing, Omar shook his head.

"I might have to report this."

Ali and Majnun reacted in unison:

"Please no."

Pulling up and zipping their pants, they slipped on shirts while Omar mused:

"I too have enjoyed the pleasures of a man, but it was not here. Not in the caliphate."

A car horn sounded twice, cutting the tension and causing Majnun and Ali to jump.

Omar looked to them:

"You still have checkpoint duty to do. Clear this car and then we can discuss the decision."

Ali rose, nervous, but grateful for the chance.

Calling the sole occupant of the vehicle over, Ali accepted the papers, examined them, and waved the man through.

Omar intervened:

"Hold on! Those are counterfeit papers!"

He stormed past Majnun and Ali and ripped down the tarp shade.

The driver started the car.

Omar raised his rifle.

Looking down the barrel, the driver saw his fate sealed. Pulling two ends of wire from under his jacket, he touched them together. Omar shot but it was too late.

The man blew up inside the car, blowing out the windows and coating the destroyed remains with a red smear.

Omar was killed near instantly. Shrapnel sliced his carotid and femoral arteries, exsanguinating him in seconds.

Majnun lie on the floor of the lean-to, still breathing but gushing blood from his abdomen.

Ali, stunned from the shockwave but unscathed, rushed to help him. Unraveling the red and white keffiyeh from around his neck, he tied it tight to Majnun's middle.

Eyeing an exit, he looked to the horizon. In it he found no escape. Three black SUVs were racing towards the checkpoint.

It was a coordinated attack.

Ali grabbed his AK and sprayed fire. Holes punched into the metal panels of the vehicles.

They kept coming.

Realizing the futility of the firefight, Ali slung his and Majnun's rifles over his shoulders and hoisted Majnun into his arms. Turning the opposite direction, he bolted towards the suburb.

Miraculously, Omar's SUV was no more than 20 meters from the other side of the barricade. Its engine was still running.

Ali made a sprint for the passenger-side door.

Laying Majnun in the passenger seat, he tossed their rifles into the back and climbed in the driver's side.

He whipped the SUV into reverse and floored it backwards towards the suburb. Achieving significant distance, Ali spun the SUV into drive and drove at max speed toward a point in the distance.

Ali had researched the place before his hajj to the caliphate.

He'd never before seen it but he knew it was there.

10

Ali raced toward the Médecins Sans Frontières hospital, no longer sure whether Majnun lie sleeping, shocked, or dead.

Omar's playlist of nasheeds provided a soundtrack for the voyage.

Pop-up signs showed that the hospital was only a few kilometers away.

At one kilometer out, Ali finally had a line-of-sight view. He feared that speeding up in a State-marked vehicle would have them shot by anyone with a rifle.

Bracing Majnun to the seat, he swerved behind the heavily-shelled skeleton of an abandoned building.

Thrusting the vehicle into park, he crossed to the passenger side, opened the door and unbuckled Majnun.

With careful haste Ali untied the bloody keffiyeh from Majnun, then peeled off Majnun's bloody shirt and his own. With bare chests, no one would mistake them for explosive martyrs. Ali wrapped the keffiyeh back into a tight, bloody belt around Majnun's midsection and readied to run.

He hefted Majnun over one shoulder- but the position put pressure on his torn skin and caused a fresh gush of blood.

Ali lowered him as quickly and gently as he could, bringing Majnun's body cradled into his arms.

Muscles and mind strained, Ali trotted with Majnun in front of him, held close to his body.

Halfway the distance his body burned. It screamed for rest but he provided none. Persevering, fueled by hope and adrenaline, Ali kept moving. His ambitious trot slowed to a labored walk. Still, he never stopped.

100 meters out, his tears started and he clenched hard on his jaw. A brief flash of despair hit him as he tried to imagine what life would be like without Majnun.

He pressed the thought from his mind by using it to propel himself forward.

30 meters from the clinic entrance, Ali started yelling:

"Help! Please! Help!"

Blood and sweat had become one. The slick coating covered their worn-out bodies.

A nurse jetted through the door. She took a second to analyze the situation- tracing her eyes up the bodies- down - then up again, before running back into the building yelling rapidly in dialect.

Ali struggled towards the door. Reaching it, he found the nurse and two male doctors waiting for him.

Their gentle strength lifted Majnun from his arms, providing relief at least to the physical burden he carried.

The nurse readied an IV as the doctors lay Majnun's body on an operating table.

She yelled questions. Her accent and the stress of the situation made them difficult to understand but Ali pressed through them.

"Bullet or bomb? Are there pieces still inside? How long ago did it happen?"

"Bomb. Probably. A few hours."

The doctors cut Ali's blood-soaked keffiyeh off of Majnun. Its red and white pattern was now soaked solid red.

"What's his blood type?"

Ali racked his brain to remember the fact that he had once known. They'd had their blood tested when they arrived at the caliphate. The answer escaped him. With tears, Ali shook his head:

"I can't remember I'm sorry I can't remember"

With sympathetic eyes, the nurse explained that Majnun would have to be blood-typed. Blood reserves were low and providing the wrong type could kill him. It'd only take a few minutes, but Majnun's pale face showed even that may be too long.

Streamed with tears and scared, Ali was punched with a blinding clarity: Majnun's blood type didn't matter. In his own veins, he carried O- blood. He could donate to any other person without complications. Ali spoke this to the woman.

Hearing it, her face replaced dread with hope.

The doctors nodded excitedly-thankful that the cause was not as lost as it had initially seemed. The nurse readied a line. She pierced a needle into the arms of both mujahideen at the same time and in seconds, Ali began transferring life.

11

Spread over hospital covers, he felt calm. No longer cold, he lay comfortably warm beneath layers of emergency blankets.

The past few hours were a blur. Bandages wrapped his abdomen and he felt tight. Still, he felt no pain.

Piecing together remnants of his day, Majnun sought to connect a recollection of working the checkpoint in Kobane to where he now lie.

A hand to his tight bandage came up wet and the magnitude of his blood loss became suddenly apparent. How was he still alive?

Back in Tunis he'd loved the sight of blood spilled over sand. The pictures in Dabiq and content channeled through Telegram excited him, aroused him, in a way. They ignited a fervor in him that inspired his journey to Kilis to join the state.

But seeing death so close and so much changed him. It forced in him the realization that death has no favorites and death holds no glory. It is merely the absence of the light that is life.

The flame of passion that he felt from being with Ali burned a thousand times brighter than the spark of hate he'd felt from viewing the images.

Since he'd experienced that glow, it became all he wanted.

Not death for anything. Only life. Only love. Only Ali.

There were no doctors or nurses nearby to tend to his queries, they were busy with new arrivals, so Majnun lay his head back and closed his eyes. His mind cycled the quandaries- turning over what he knew and what he wondered.

Ali rested tucked in a corner of the clinic's lounge.

He'd put three units of blood into Majnun, a dangerous amount.

A saline drip replaced some of his lost fluids, still he felt weak.

He'd offered more but the doctors refused to take it, saying it'd kill him without even guaranteeing life for Majnun.

The doctors had stopped the bleeding and stabilized him, now Majnun's fate rested in Allah's hands.

To Ali, the doctors prescribed sleep and food. Donations from a Bedouin herdsmen brought goats milk, yogurt, kefir, and eggs to the hospital. Absent any semblance of an appetite, Ali forced himself to consume- intent on refilling his protein, in case additional blood donations became necessary.

With a full stomach, a warm haze engulfed Ali, drifting his mind far from the couch he lie on.

The next dozens of hours passed
cautiously.

Slowly, it became clear that
Majnun would survive the attack.

As soon as his strength
returned enough to support visitors,
Ali came to his curtain covey.

"I wanted to come back sooner
but they said you needed rest. That
we both needed rest."

Majnun met Ali's eyes with
gratitude:

"What happened? How did we get
here?"

"Jabhat al-Nusra attacked the
checkpoint. There was a suicide
blast. Omar was killed. There were
too many of them. I couldn't hold
them off so I drove you here."

"Where is here?"

"A Médecins Sans Frontières
international hospital."

Majnun smiled at the innocent
dismissiveness in Ali's response.

"How were we not on shot on
sight?"

Ali took a seat next to Majnun
on the hospital cot.

"I carried you for the last
kilometer; shirtless- so they
wouldn't mistake us for martyrs."

Majnun wondered over the feat:

"Thank you."

"They said they'd release us soon-"

Ali traced his hand from Majnun's blood and bandage covered abs up to his bare chest. He covered Majnun's heart with an open palm.

"-You lost a lot of blood."

Majnun's eyes broke from Ali's hand to meet Ali's.

"How did I survive?"

Ali flipped his arm to reveal veins scarred with needle tracks.

"I gave you life."

Majnun's eyes welled.

"I wish I didn't have to take from you; to grow strong as you grow weak."

"I would give everything I have to be with you."

Majnun knew it to be truth, though a small part of him wished it wasn't.

Ali brought his forehead to Majnun's and Majnun raised his to meet it.

Wincing, Majnun drew back in pain. Reflexively, Ali braced his hands to Majnun's sides and held them there.

"You're still hurt. We should stay longer."

"I'm fine. We should go as soon as we can."

"You're not."

"I am. We should leave soon. The longer we stay from the state, the more suspicious it will be when we return."

Ali knew the statement to be an unfortunate fact. With resign, he rested against Majnun- packed tight to the hospital cot.

They stayed there together until a warm-eyed doctor woke Ali.

"You need real sleep. Not crammed together on one of these tiny beds. They're too small almost for one person. How about that spot you like in the lounge area?"

Walking together, they left Majnun's bed. Out of earshot, Ali asked:

"We need to leave soon- my friend is still in a lot of pain- is there anything you can do?"

With a sigh, the doctor explained:

"I'm sorry, supplies are so low. We barely have enough to treat the patients we have now and we have new arrivals every day."

With pleading eyes, Ali explained briefly the unique predicament he found himself in.

The sympathy the doctor drew from the story showed in his face.

He put one finger in the air, left, and returned a moment later.

This is all I can spare. I can't even really spare this, donations are down, but… You need it."

The doctor held out a small vial of morphine and two syringes, bundled together with Médecins Sans Frontières tape.

"Shukran."

"Salaam Alaikum son. You're cleared to go first thing tomorrow. Just please get some sleep first."

The kind doctor motioned to the bed and Ali lied down.

"Shukran."

14

Tucked away in the expansive bedrooms, Majnun and Ali lived another happy eternity together. Free from the bonds of the State, their bond to each other strengthened.

The olive trees outside grew lusher and fuller, their prosperity in bounty.

But on the horizon a storm brewed. It started as whispers of wind, unfelt from within.

Unanswered it grew. Leaves from the trees whipped around.

Rainbows and blue skies were killed by dark grey clouds.

Cool set in the air.

Thunder or artillery rumbled in the distance. Lightning shattered the soft. Paradise was plunged into chaos.

The cyclone kept growing until the trees themselves whipped wildly in the whirlwind.

Inside, the children grew scared.

Majnun covered the door with a bookshelf and Ali covered the door with another.

The lights flickered and then went black. Ali felt to find a lantern in the darkness. He lit it and together they huddled around its warm glow.

The storm outside intensified. It howled like the jet engines of fighter planes. Rain and hail cut leaves from the trees.

One tree became weak. Its branches bowed to the force of the gusts, but its intertwined partner would not allow it to break.

They stooped under the weight of water and wind, but still held strong.

Books knocked from the shelves as they shook. Hail pounded on the roof, banging down fury.

"Leave with #11! Take them and go! You can get away!"

Majnun yelled the directions to Ali, knowing the vehicle wasn't large enough to carry them both with the children.

"No! I will not leave you! This is our home! We can survive this together!"

Ali made no habit of defying Majnun, but the idea of leaving him behind was disgusting.

Majnun tried to force the key to #11 into Ali's hand but he would not accept it.

Instead, Ali stacked mattresses against the bookshelves to block the door and window. For added weight, he hefted the dressers over.

Still the storm fought back.

Outside a branch snapped and fell to the ground, impacting the car and setting off the alarm.

Inside, greater terrors drew near.

Pounding on the door and window added cacophony to the screams of wind and hammering of rain and hail.

Growling with might, masked men broke down the barricades. Long dirty beards peeked out from black masks and colorless eyes.

"Go!" insisted Majnun. "Leave with the children! You can make it out alive!"

Ali turned to see a new door along the back wall- or maybe it was there the whole time and he just didn't notice.

Ali looked at the children, then hesitated back to Majnun:

"I can't leave without you."

"You can"

"I won't."

Majnun knew it was true but wished otherwise.

Together they fought side-by-side for their futures and those of their children.

They exerted every ounce of effort within themselves to combat the intruders.
Still they kept coming.

Ali woke just as daylight was starting to creep into the long night.

He arrived at Majnun's section, expecting to have to wake him up, but found him already awake.

"We're cleared to go."

"Yeah the doctor told me."

Ali nodded in thought, then stooped down to help Majnun to his feet.

No longer strong enough to carry Majnun, Ali braced their bodies together and they carried each other. Through the ward and check-in area, out to the heat of the desert.

They walked the kilometer in twice the time it took Ali alone. The SUV was still where Ali parked it; passenger seat still damp despite the desert air.

"We should leave the State."

Majnun spoke the first words in hours.

Ali sat up surprised, having assumed his companion was still asleep. Struggling for a response, he finally managed:

"Why?"

Majnun continued, with eyes still closed:

"There lies a land beyond the Caliphate. We could go there together."

"And leave the Jihad?"

"We've fought bravely in the name of Allah; I think he would forgive us if we took a break."

"And the girls?"

"They're smart girls, they could make it out alive, maybe even with one of those cars we saw in Kobane."

Majnun spoke the words, wishing to believe them.

Ali countered: "It'd be suspicious to the Turks or Kurds if we left without them."

"But it'd be suspicious to the State if we left with them. We should just quit while we're ahead."

Ali took a concerned look at Majnun's abdomen:

"Are we really ahead?"

Majnun flashed a quick smile at the gentle bluntness in Ali's question.

"I mean quit before we're more behind. I survived this, hamdulillah, because of you."

"And you will survive next time because of me."

"But what if I just get you killed?"

"Brother, you wouldn't do so. I know you wouldn't."

"What if I can't help it? What if something just happens and you die because of me?"

"Then I would die with you by my side. I have your back and you have mine."

The words hung in the air until their sentiment grew stale. Neither mujahid rushed to continue the topic, preferring instead to evanesce their existence into the groves of olives they passed.

The tranquil uniformity in their surroundings lulled a calm and Ali and Majnun that they had not felt since before Tabqa. Before things got out of control.

Ali was the first to see it. Just past the end of the grove- a checkpoint dotted with the black flag.

It lie intentionally obfuscated, unable to be seen until it was too late- a common state tactic.

Turning around and driving away would be taken akin to a guilty verdict- triggering a barrage of bullets at their vehicle.

With no other options, Ali pulled into the queue behind the other unwitting motorists.

17

In the still silence of the queue, Ali and Majnun sat with the engine off- standard State protocol.

 With their windows down, they hushed out a plan and whispered quiet confidences to each other.

One at a time, the cars ahead of them were cleared and Ali drove slowly forward.

"Follow my lead."

"Always."

Reaching the front, they were met with immediately suspicious eyes, something they hoped to avoid in a State vehicle.

"Papers please."

The guard's tone didn't extend his pleasantry.

"I'm sorry brother, we don't have papers. We got attacked in Kobane and we're just trying to get back there."

"No papers, no problem. Just pop the trunk and hood and we can get you cleared to be on your way."

The man smiled tensely, motioning to the other guard has he spoke. The guard circled to the rear of the vehicle.

Majnun recognized immediately the maneuver taking place.

"If you need proof, find it with Abu Shami in Kobane."

The guard slammed his hand on the trunk, unimpressed. The rear guard raised his rifle.

"Or Commander Azazi at Tabqa Airbase!"

The hostile guard's expression flipped, first to curious, then suspicious.

"Lies. You are spies. The Dawlah does not control Tabqa. You are dogs of Bashar."

Ali jumped in to counter:

"We did not risk martyrdom, and watch our brother attain it, to be called lying spying dogs."

Reading the veritas in Ali's statement, the man eased. An excited smile attempted to conceal the fact that he nearly murdered both of them.

"So it's true then? Tabqa belongs to the state? Mashallah."

Majnun nodded and Ali replied smoothly:

"She does. She came at the cost of the blood of many martyrs but she is a beauty to be seen."

Both guards erupted into spontaneous Takbir:

"Allahu Akbar!"

The guard invited Majnun and Ali to step out of the vehicle and they complied- unsure of the optionality of the invitation. `

With a fake smile and extended hand, the guard introduced himself simply as Bin Muhammad. The rear guard remained silent.

"My apologies-" said Bin Muhammad, waving his hand through the air as if to wave off the issue. "-We've been living disparate from reliable news of the State. Communications lines and electricity have been cut, so we've been living in the way of the Prophet, peace be upon him."

Majnun cracked a smile at the joke before realizing it wasn't one.

Ali smiled too and with a cool tone of voice replied:

"No problem brother. You are forgiven. We are just looking to pass through to Kobane-" he paused with tactful effect "-We were working a checkpoint there when a Nusra attack injured my partner-" he motioned to Majnun, who lifted his shirt to reveal the gauzed gore underneath.

Bin Muhammad looked with shocked intrigue.

"Apologies again brothers. Mashallah- you are still alive."

"Mashallah" Ali and Majnun replied in unison.

"I would be happy to escort you to Raqqa to obtain new travel documents."

Ali suaved:

"Thank you brother but we must decline. We must be back in Kobane soon and we can secure the documents ourselves when we arrive."

Bin Muhammad stared through without a response.

Majnun jumped in to salvage the situation:

"Pardon his haste, we've left our virgin brides in Kobane."

"You've yet to taste the fruit of your virgin wives?"

Ali smiled: "A taste so sweet needs to be savored with a celebration."

"A trip to Raqqa would merit such a celebration. She's one of the State's greatest achievements. I can have my men retrieve your wives and meet us at the courthouse while we're getting your papers."

Ali hesitated, then revealed:

"The checkpoint we were working was likely captured by Jabhat al-Nusra after we were attacked."

"I'll have a team of my best mujahideen assembled to wrest it from the hands of the Nusra dogs."

"Perhaps we should give until morning and then look to Raqqa with fresh eyes."

"Nonsense, I can drive you and you can regain them on the way."

Realizing they weren't going to be able to suave their way out of the situation, Ali capitulated the GPS coordinates of the house the girls were staying at and Majnun showed the code knock- repeated several times for memory.

Bin Muhammad looked to the still-nameless rear guard to ensure comprehension. Finding it, he lined out plans for the assault and a list of names to be assembled.

As he turned to leave, Majnun stopped the man. Reaching out a hand, he slipped away the rest of his blister pack of Captagon.

"If our wives' purity is not intact, it will be your and your men's death writs I seek in Raqqa."

Similarly, Ali pushed his pills off to Bin Muhammad"

"Ensure the fruit remains unspoiled."

Bin Muhammad looked to the rear guard's eyes and nodded:

"They will be waiting for us in Raqqa."

Leaving Omar's SUV parked in the queue, Ali and Majnun loaded into an SUV with Bin Muhammad.

Bin Muhammad started the engine and bounced on the Toyota's horn until another guard came running out from the checkpoint.

Together, the four of them set out for their journey to Raqqa.

18

The courthouse lie in the center of Raqqa proper. Cars passed and pedestrians walked as civilians tried to preserve the normalcy in their day.

Bin Muhammad's SUV rolled to a stop on the street outside of the courthouse. Levering the door handles, Majnun and Ali found them locked, suddenly realizing they had been locked in for the duration of their voyage.

"My mistake!" Bin Muhammad said, flashing another fake smile and opening the door from the outside.

"Welcome to Raqqa."

Ali sprang forth and stretched his legs and Majnun followed through the same door.

Seeing the State insignia, citizens of the Caliphate averted their eyes.

Bin Muhammad led Majnun and Ali inside, the other escorting guard followed from the rear. At the door a decree was posted, requiring all defendants to surrender their weapons before entering. With reluctance, Majnun and Ali complied.

The artificiality of design of the interior of the courthouse stung with contrast to the authenticity of the doctrine it held to proclaim.

Long lines snaked the length of the building- a commonality Ali and Majnun had come to expect throughout the Caliphate.

Bin Muhammad led them to a queue, spoke a few quiet words to their rear guard, and strode off.

On hearing the words, the guard subconsciously bumped his rifle and flashed a quick smile. Realizing he was being watched, he jumped into an over-elated examination of the courthouse:

"She's beautiful- a testament to the greatness of the State- finally justice can be dispensed in the way of Allah."

Majnun smiled tensely and Ali replied:

"Certainly a sight to be seen."

The sarcasm of the statement lost on the guard, he lit up in Takbir:

"Allahu Akbar!"

For the next few minutes, Majnun and Ali stood silently, still uncertain of their fate but thankful for the relief from forced conversation with their apparent captor.

Soon, Bin Muhammad returned with two serious-looking court guards.

Turning to Ali and Majnun, he spoke:

"There were complications in retaking the checkpoint. Several of my men- our men- have been wounded or martyred in the process. Rest assured however that you will see your wives as soon as it's back under State control.

Ali and Majnun thanked the man with the first genuine gratitude they'd given.

Bin Muhammad smiled his first genuine smile, exchanged "Salaams" with the pair of mujahideen, and left with the rear guard.

Gradually their relative position in line reduced with their new guards never far away.

Eventually, they were no longer waiting in the lobby, but in a courthouse presided over by a mufti in flowing white robe. He delivered verdicts and decrees with hasty determine, quickly clearing the way between Majnun and Ali and the podiums at the front of the courtroom.

Directly in front of the judge, Majnun spoke:

"We were fighters at Tabqa, then served the Jihad at a checkpoint in Kobane. I was injured and my brother in Allah took me to the international hospital to be treated."

He motioned to Ali, then pulled up his shirt to reveal the bloody bandages. He continued:

"If you need verification, you can find it with Commander Abu Shami in Kobane, or Commander Mustafa Azazi at Tabqa Airbase."

The Mufti raised his eyes at Majnun's performance, then turned to the guards.

"Have you received word from Commander Shami or Commander Azazi?"

One guard spoke up:

"Abu Shami has been removed from his position as a result of his failure to totally neutralize enemy populations."

The Mufti shook his head with dismay and looked to the second guard.

"Commander Azazi has spoken highly of these muharibūn and has invited them to return to Tabqa, if they require an assignment."

The judge smiled.

"Excellent, here are two new identification writs-"

He handed two pages of paper to the guard, who handed them to Majnun and Ali.

"-Please fill them out and I can officially welcome you back to the State."

Providing the pertinent information, they handed them back to the guard, who handed them to the Mufti.

"One more thing, from your grace-" started Majnun, reading the expressions of the guards as he did.

"-Our wives in Kobane will be delivered here soon. They are both with child, and I'd like them to take the good news to my sister in Kurdish-held territory."

The Mufti stooped his eyes to meet Majnun's.

"Is your sister sympathetic to the State?"

"Yes your honor."

"Do you plan to travel with them?"

"No."

"When do they plan to return?"

"Within three days. No more."

The Mufti smiled, first at Majnun, then at Ali.

"Congratulations lions."

He flipped through pages on his desk- signed two- and handed them

off to the guard, whose affect remained unchanged throughout.
Ali and Majnun exchanged "Salaams" and "Shukrans" with the judge, and their hearing was over- thankfully easier than they'd expected.


Ali and Majnun spent the next few hours in the courthouse lobby, watching lines of nervous people stream past. Relieved to now be documented, they rested lazily against each other, waiting for the girls to arrive.

A small group of mujahideen moved up to them, the foremost carried their rifles- one in each hand.
Majnun and Ali sat up with small smiles, content with the acceptance they were finally receiving.
The man offered their rifles and spoke:
"Two more mujahideen are needed to participate in an execution. I would like you to be those two mujahideen."
Ali and Majnun accepted the rifles with dismay; it was impossible to decline.

19

Three SUV's parked in a convoy
outside of the courthouse carried
them immediately to their
destination.

The ride was short and tense.

The beige-tan brick building,
occupied by a textile company before
the war, towered above them-
unassuming but for the crowd
gathered under it.

Masked mujahideen milled about
militarily, keeping the crowd
corralled.

As they brushed past, a guard
from the convoy announced that
instead of using the elevator, the
condemned would be forced to walk up
the stairs- to bear testament to the
complete consequence of sinning
against Allah.

In reality, a lack of electric
flow necessitated it. State
occupation had crippled even basic
services in Raqqa, plunging areas
into rolling or total blackouts.

The crowd knew this but cheered
anyway- motivated by fear of
repercussion.

Satisfied, the fighter strode
contentedly ahead, quickly sold on
his own lie.

Ascending, Majnun focused on counting each step as he took it, forcing the number into his mind. Still, at the top, he had no idea how many they'd taken.

Ali focused solely on Majnun.

It was windier six stories above Raqqa than below. Still, the breeze provided little respite from the heat of the situation.

The two accused men were forced to the edge of the building nearest the crowd. Amplified by a megaphone, the allegations against them were recited. Through them, their eyes never left each other's.

They mirrored into each other with fiery audacity, struck by fear but filled with love.

Finally, the mujahid delivered his Sharia prescription: Death.

At the word, the men wavered-looking around to meet all the eyes of those who condemned them.

Majnun attempted to convey a look of sympathy, but stopped when he realized what it alone was worth.

For theatrics the fighter continued:

"Child of Lot. Abomination of Sodom. You have sinned against Allah and made foul the message brought by his Prophet, Muhammad, peace be upon him. Now you will pay the price."

One of the men broke:

"Forgive me! Allah forgive me!"

The masked mujahid paused, as if to contemplate the comment.

"Allah may forgive you, but you will have to ask him directly."

With a swift push, he sent the man sailing over the side. Air swallowed into his lungs, stealing the sounds before he could make them.

Six stories below, a fleshy smack announced his arrival.

The second man pressed for every inch of the barrier wall separating solid surface from the edge. Now, seeing his fate totally sealed, he flung himself over, in search of a quick death.

He did not find it.

He landed as the first man, with a thick splat, but still he retained consciousness.

Legs lying limp, he dragged himself to the body of his companion.

Resting the man's bloody head into his arms, he kissed it tenderly.

"WITNESS THE ABOMINATION!"

One of the masked guards roared from below, casting a stone at the mangled men.

It missed, but triggered a more violently accurate stone barrage.

Forced at gunpoint, several civilians joined in- halt-heartedly lobbing broken cinder at the couple.

From six stories above, Ali peered with disgust. Empathy for the man pulled his sidearm from its holster and one perfect shot instantly ended the torment.

With the exception of Majnun, all the mujahideen on the rooftop shot Ali dirty looks. Still, they didn't question his action. Even they had begun to ponder the amount of brutality that a regime can inflict while still maintaining a loyal populace.

20

At the base of the building, the crowd had begun to disperse. Ali looked with disgust at the wasted bodies of the two men. Majnun looked at the ground.

The convoy of SUV's waited to carry them back to the courthouse. Arriving there near dark, the courthouse was closed for the day.

Ali and Majnun took seats on the steps. The rest of the guards cleared and they were left to contemplate the day's occurrences alone.

They sat in silence.

Over an hour later, another convoy of trucks and SUV's pulled up. A man they recognized as the rear guard from the checkpoint stepped out.

He opened the back door and from it crawled their wives.

"They were surviving only on chocolate when we found them." The rear guard spoke to Majnun and Ali.

Their wives walked to stand by their sides, fear in their eyes began to fade upon the happiness of seeing their husbands.

"And Hamdi?" Asked Majnun.

The guard paused quizzically, then nodded and spoke solemnly:

"The bodies of two of our mujahideen were found near the checkpoint, only meters from each other."

Ali and Majnun met each other's eyes with sadness.

"I am sorry to have to bring that bad news. However, I also come with good: Bin Muhammad has arranged an apartment for you here in Raqqa. I would be happy to take you there."

Too tired to object, Majnun and Ali piled back into the back of the SUV with their wives.

The group of SUV's brought them to a block apartment reminiscent of Soviet structure.

Opening the door, the guard let Majnun and Ali and their wives out.

Without a word, he led them inside and up to an apartment. Twisting the handle, he opened the unlocked door and led the group inside.

"Feel free to stay here until your next assignment. Bin Muhammad sends his regards."

The apartment looked like someone had recently been living in it. Belongings made it feel almost like home.

    "Salaam Alaikum lions, enjoy
your stay here in Raqqa."
    Then, the nameless man left.
    "Home" smiled Ali.
    Majnun looked around the room
then reluctantly accepted the
invitation in Ali's eyes.
    "Home."

Ali and Majnun got the girls set up
in the living room with pillows and
blankets. Then, after making sure
they were well fed with food from
the kitchen, they retreated to the
sole bedroom for the night.

21

It was dark. Not the dark of night, but the kind of eerie twilight that sometimes occurs before or after heavy rains.

A sound darker than the ambiance cut it.

A man was screaming. Not shouts of anger or wails of sadness, but screams of genuine pain.

Black smoke and shelled-out vehicles lay littered in the streets.

Ali recognized the town of Tal Hamis from the windows of the police station he was in.

Although he and Majnun joined the State in Kilis, and became trained in the desert, this is where they first saw real action. It tested them.

The initial assault on Tal Hamis had gone as expected- easier even. It was the blitz counterattack that caught them by surprise. It weighed their value as mujahideen.

Government and Kurdish forces, frustrated by recent State successes, launched a counterattack intended to make a hard push to the center of the city. The win would bear strategic interest and propaganda value. This coveted combination made strange bedfellows into enemies of Majnun and Ali.

The assault had pounded the police station. One-by-one mujahideen fell, until only Majnun and Ali were left unscathed. Ali sprayed fire from the front of the police station and prayed to Allah that he would not be martyred that day. Majnun ran behind him and Ali wondered if he was leaving- running away. He wouldn't have blamed him for it, the situation was hopeless.

But Majnun did not flee. Within a minute he was back:

"Brother! This way!"

Ali followed. Together they ran out a hidden exit off the back of the building.

That day proved their bond more than words. They really would be there for each other.


The police station bore scars of the assault.

It was almost odd to be in this place without bullets coming at him. Even with the man's pained screams, it had never been this quiet.

Ali rounded to the back exit and found Majnun coming towards him.

"Come on" hushed Majnun. "This way"

Ali followed.

The eerie dark made them yearn for the relative comfort of the police station but they pressed onward toward the source of the screaming.

The sight of it made them wish they hadn't.

In the middle of a street off the city square, a man hung suspended- mounted to a cross.

With the thought of helping the man, they moved closer.

The weird twilight made him difficult to see.

Mere meters from the base of the cross, Majnun finally recognized the man.

"Abu Shami"

Abu Shami didn't respond. He continued to scream in agony. Nails pierced through his hands and feet oozed streams of blood. The Ba'athist emblems from his military uniform were now sewn into his skin. They too oozed. Across his chest burned a brand: "King Of The Kurds"

Transfixed on this horror, Majnun and Ali didn't see the masked men coming towards them until they were already surrounded.

Without their rifles or sidearms, Ali and Majnun raised

their fists in preparation of the fight.

They never found it.

Shots cracked through the streets, incapacitating the nearest masked men.

Ali searched for the shooter:
"There!"

On the roof of an adjacent building, a woman in military garb perched with a Dragunov sniper. She waved a hand signal and an engine revved.

Plowing through the crowd came a pickup truck with two women in the cab, also in military uniform. Yellow patches on their jackets identified them as YPJ- The Kurdish women's fighting force.

Their eyes spoke "Get in" so Majnun and Ali obeyed, hopping into the bed of the truck.

The truck sped off and they were safe for a moment.

Majnun was the first to recognize the faces of their rescuers. Knocking on the back window of the cab, he confirmed it.

It was the girls. They turned to Majnun and Ali, waved, and flashed slight sly smiles.

Ali and Majnun smiled incredulously back.

They flew onward, accelerating continuously. Updrafts from their speed caused the truck to start to lift. Still the girls sped toward safety.

.Winds whipped and dark clouds rushed ahead of them.

The closer they grew to freedom, the more powerful the gusts became.

A bump in the road sent Majnun airborne. Ali grabbed his hand and he too was sent up.

They shouted for the girls to stop but no sounds came out. The girls blazed onward to safety.

Majnun and Ali were sucked up into the currents and tossed mercilessly. Hail stones pelted them and their grip on each other broke.

No longer gaining altitude, they began to fall. Reaching for the comfort of each other, they found it just out of reach.

The ground under them became visible again. On it, dots of blacks moved toward the place they would be landing.

They hoped only for a quick death.

In the soft bed, Ali and Majnun woke up hard against each other.

Majnun awoke disturbed, with the desire to press the dream from his mind.

Taking advantage of the apartment's amenities, he stood in a long hot shower to cleanse his body and mind.

Ali came in and met Majnun under the warm water. He pushed his lips to the back of Majnun's neck, then ran his hands over the warm stream flowing down Majnun's chest and abs. Tracing his fingers down the trail of hair, he embraced Majnun with one hand and cupped him with the other.

Majnun grew aroused but pulled Ali's hands away.

"No. Leave"

"What?"

"Go-" commanded Majnun "-To Mosul or Palmyra, Aleppo, Hama, or Idlib. It doesn't matter where, just that you leave and I never see you again."

Ali stood stunned, his happy demeanor wiped away and replaced with shock and angst.

"Brother why are you being so cruel?"

Majnun spat back at him:

"Cruel? You don't know the meaning of the word."

"But brother, our love" Ali pleaded dejectedly.

Majnun stared back at him with equal contempt and disgust.

"Our love? How can you be so stupid? Our love is on a rooftop in Raqqa and six stories below it. We can't have love here. Sneaking minutes in tents and trucks and shelled out houses? Fighting futility to keep it boxed off from the world, until we fail, and someone sees us, and it's us being sacrificed to the pavement?"

"So we can leave!" Argued Ali. "Go someplace far away from here so we can be together."

"How?" Countered Majnun. "Where? Even if we managed to escape State territory and trick our way past the Turks or Iraqis? Then what? We could never get to the west. The only countries where we could have that love won't have us. We're the enemies. We burned our passports. Renounced our citizenship. We're stuck here. This hell. This caliphate-" he said the word with loathing "It is our only home now, and it is a home we cannot inhabit together."

Ali's face had gone from shocked to pained. He desired to tell Majnun that everything he had just said was false, but he knew it wasn't. The tears he'd fought to hold back began streaming down his face.

"But brother, I love you. I can't exist without you."

Ali could offer no other argument. He lay his feelings bare in the simplest terms he could, hoping that hearing them, Majnun would realize he was right, that they did belong together, that they could.

But Majnun remained steadfast in his scathing:

"You love to be as the Sodomites. That is all. You seek physical pleasure. That is all we had. Nothing more. Not love."

Majnun didn't believe the words as he said them, but hoped saying them would make him believe. He didn't. Hearing the words out loud just made him repulsed by them more. He tried to embrace the sentiment, the lies he told. He couldn't. That's all they were, lies. He and Ali had shared something real and wholly beautiful. Something that made life worth living, even in this forsaken Caliphate.

But from the beginning it hinged in impossibility. Even while they shared it, they knew that a love so fragile could never last.

In theory, their lives could transcend each other, they could relegate each other to distant faint memories of the past. Just as in theory, one could give up the sun and subject themselves only to darkness.

But what difference is day or night in the absence of the sun? What difference life or death?

23

Ali racked his brain, trying to think of a way that he and Majnun could be happy together. He searched for an irrefutable idea, something he could take to Majnun that he'd have no choice but to accept.

Still he kept coming up blank-every thought path had its own fatalistic flaw.

The longer he thought on it, the more convinced he became that Majnun was right.

They'd both spent the last money they had just to reach Kilis.

They had no family left, at least none that would communicate with them.

They had no lives to return to.

Their hejira to the Caliphate, since the beginning, was planned to be only one-way.

The State had cultivated so much animosity through its brutality that Ali and Majnun could not expect to be treated as prisoners-of-war, but as a plague- to be purged lest it should spread.

Defeated, Ali held his head in his hands and cried. Majnun couldn't make the tears stop. He'd been gone all day. Maybe he left for good. The situation was hopeless.

Before he came to the state, Ali felt empty inside. He craved a spark. Something to make him feel. And he found it. Not in the glory and gore of the battlefield, but in the heart of Majnun.

In tears, Ali lamented the fact that the State that brought them together was now the driving force tearing them apart. He yearned for a way to separate his love with Majnun from the death and destruction of the Caliphate, but found the two too intrinsically linked.

24

Majnun paced quickly through the streets of Raqqa. He had hoped the walk would help clear his mind but it only added confusion. As his feet carried him past closed food stands and burqa-clad women, his mind stayed fixed on Ali.

His surroundings blurred together in the hot humid summer haze. He quickened his steps with no destination in mind.

He tried so hard to make Ali leave. Why wouldn't he just go?

His feet pounded the pavement, streaks of light and movement passed in his peripheries.

Why wouldn't Ali depart? If not to save himself, then to save them both. If Ali would leave, they would both be set free.

Had his scathing not been enough to convey the message? It was selfish almost in a way, for Ali to stay. To do such a thing- to doom them both.

Majnun stopped in the thought. He commanded cruelty to drive Ali away while he himself stayed. He could just as easily leave as Ali. Majnun looked at his feet, then around the unfamiliar streets. He didn't know where he was, but he knew where he was going.

25

Majnun burst through the apartment door in a full sweat.

Ali and the girls jolted up from their seats on the living room couches at the sudden intrusion.

Ali greeted Majnun excitedly:

"Brother!"

Before resignedly admitting:

"You were right."

Majnun nodded slightly directly to Ali's eyes but didn't vocalize an acknowledgment.

"I was unnecessarily cruel to you. You've shown me only love for the entire time I've known you and I responded with hate."

"I forgive you."

Majnun continued: "I tried to drive you away while I myself was not strong enough to leave."

Tears started flowing on all faces in the room.

Majnun opened his arms for an embrace from Ali and Ali met them.

"Brother I don't want to live in the fear that our love will get us killed."

Majnun lifted his head off Ali's shoulders and met his red eyes.

"We don't have to live in fear."

Detaching from Ali, Majnun moved toward the bedroom. He was back in less than a minute with his backpack, unzipping all the pockets and gathering small stashes of cash into one pile.

Reading his lead, Ali grabbed his own bag and added his bills to the cache. It totaled a small stack of Syrian Pounds, Turkish Lira, Iraqi Dinar and American Dollars.

Content with it, Majnun retrieved his AK, pressed his thumb to the metal hole on its butt plate and pulled out the metallic cylinder from within. Then, turning to Ali and the girls, he spoke:

"Let's go."

Hailing a cab from in front of the apartment building, the group loaded in. Majnun peeled an American $20 from the stack.

"Take us to the desert north of the city. Somewhere quiet."

The driver accepted the bill, nodded, and began driving.

"Listen" Majnun said to the girls.

"You're leaving us."

He popped open the metal capsule and pulled out the girls'

travel writs and two USB sticks- one green and one red.

Majnun held up the red USB drive:

"Present this to the Kurds. It has actionable, tactical information that they will find useful. It will grant you safe passage to Erbil."

Holding up the green USB drive, Majnun continued:

"Do not speak of this to the Kurds. When you get to Erbil, contact the US Consulate. They'll guide you through what to do. This contains information on the State's oil and antiquities trade that the Americans will find useful. Do not give out that information until they come to collect it. It is your only leverage and your ticket out."

Ali's eyes shimmered with genuine incredulity:

"How?"

"At Tabqa, before Azazi gave me the news of our transfer to Kobane, he asked me to make a back-up of his porn collection because he was afraid that the 'Kuffar dogs would try to castrate his desires.'"

Majnun mocked air-quotes as he spoke the words with his best Azazi impersonation.

Ali and the girls laughed so hard that even the driver joined in with empathetic chuckles.

"Here is good and quiet" the driver said as they pulled up to a town just north of Raqqa.

Majnun pulled an American $50 bill from the stack and thanking the man, the group climbed out of the car. As its headlights faded into the distance, Majnun handed the remaining cash to the girls and pointed north.

"That way. Walk until you make it to Kurdish areas. You know what to do then. Understand?"

The girls nodded and spoke the only word Majnun and Ali had ever heard from them:

"Shukran."

With that, they turned to leave.

Ali stopped them:

"Wait. You must say you escaped from us. If you say you escaped your Daesh husbands, you will be met with open arms. If you say you were sent by them, it will be closed fists. Understand?"

The girls again nodded and repeated the one word:

"Shukran."

With that, they turned, laced fingers, and left.

Now entirely penniless, Majnun and Ali turned and laced their fingers for their walk back to Raqqa.

Stars in the desert sky spoke of a land beyond the Caliphate. Under them, Majnun and Ali spoke of their plan within it.

Mid-morning, Ali and Majnun arrived back at their apartment. Gathering their packs and rifles, they set out on their walk to the center of Raqqa proper.

They arrived at the courthouse at noon. Telling the door guards of their desire to return to Tabqa, they were directed toward a group of mujahideen who were organizing a convoy.

The apparent leader of the group confirmed that seats were still available and invited Majnun and Ali to fill them.

After an uncomfortable ride, Ali and Majnun entered Tabqa in a vehicle for the second time. This time with less drama, but still all of the tension of the first.

Ali's arm, propped against Majnun, provided only a small comfort in the tense moment.

Upon its arrival, Commander Azazi greeted the convoy. Recognizing familiar faces, he asked Majnun and Ali:

"Lions! Where are your brides?"

"Sold-" replied Majnun "-and the money sent to our families."

Ali nodded and Azazi laughed:

"Personally I would have chosen to keep them longer, but perhaps you made a prudent financial decision."

Ali and Majnun smiled through their disgust and Azazi wandered off to meet the leader of Mosul front, there to help coordinate the assault on Damascus.

Making pace over the familiar territory, Ali and Majnun continued to the Operations Room to sign up for their missions. They knew the background checks may take a day or two, but were sure they would be approved.

Ali and Majnun spent much of the next hours praying and reading the Qur'an.

Reading and reciting the words, they reminisced over what they meant before coming to the Dawlah, and what they meant now.

Most of the morning leading up to their missions, Ali and Majnun stayed separate.

Right before they were to be loaded into separate trucks, they met each other at the barracks building they'd helped claim. It wasn't planned, they just knew they would find each other there.

Seeing each other they smiled, cried, hugged, and kissed.

Majnun pulled the MSF morphine bundle from his pocket and unstuck one syringe from the tape. Rolling up Ali's sleeve, he injected the lion's share of the liquid. With the same needle, he emptied the bottle into his own arm.

The morphine sent a rush through them and they embraced. It felt like the first time they met.

"I love you."

"And I you."

"And I had you."
"You will always have me."

   With those words, the pair of
mujahideen tearfully parted toward
their own separate destinations.

29

Ten meters below the Operations Room, regional commanders from across the Caliphate had begun to gather to plan the assault on Damascus. Preliminary attacks were to begin at dusk, with first-round blitzes continuing through the night.

Commander Azazi, ever paranoid, demanded a radio unit be installed in the bunker, to ensure the group would never be out of contact. The microphone receiver sat idly on the box- unplugged to prevent obtrusive listening.

As the sun set a story above, the seats at the block of tables filled near completely with commanders. It was rumored that Abu Bakr Al-Baghdadi would be in attendance, though no one had yet seen the elusive man.

At dusk, a "go-ahead" order was issued for the semi-trucks at the front of the column. Packed with explosives, the trucks were to provide the initial punch needed to breach the Government's defenses and clear the way for waves of shock troops.

Radio chatter speckled through the sweaty room, confirming receipt of the commands and conveying the departure of the semis. Content, Commander Azazi gruffed his way to a map board at the front of the room. With sweeping motions, he indicated the Dawlah forces and showed their planned strategy for the first round of assaults. Mid-explanation, Azazi was interrupted by a voice on the radio speaking clearly with slight concern:

"One of the fore-assault trucks is inbound back to base."

"Mechanical issues probably." Replied one voice.

"Did you check the fuel levels?" Asked another

"Fuel levels were fine. The driver's hands were left untaped. He should be able to resolve any issues himself."

"Untaped?"

"Yes, the driver expressed his desire to raise his hands to Allah at the moment of impact. He is a loyal and pious mujahid. Something must be wrong."

A new voice piped through the air:

"You were at the South gate send-off? You should have told me you were here."

"I was not at the South gate…
This is not a truck from my column."

The words hung on the airwaves
for a second, then:

"I have a truck approaching the
South gate as well-"

The roar of a horn over the
radio cut off the man's words. Less
than a second later, the full sound
became audible from the bunker.

Commander Azazi was the first
to piece together what was
happening. Barreling across the
room, he fumbled to connect the
microphone to the transmitter- then
shouted into it:

"STOP THE TRUCKS! Ready a TOW
missile or RPG! Use your rifles! Or
your sidearms! Throw rocks if you
have to! JUST STOP-"

An explosion rumbled through
the base, cutting off Azazi's words.

Majnun saw the explosion before
he heard it. He smiled. Ali had
reached paradise.
A second later, he joined him.

Salaam Alaikum-

Although this is a work of fiction, care was emphasized in accurately portraying events in the Syrian Civil War as a whole. The capture and massacre at Tabqa, use of child brides as rewards for battlefield achievements, and execution for sexual offenses are all unfortunate products of the conflict at the hands of ISIS.

Place names were chosen for use with the most commonly used translations/transliterations. This was done for clarity.

The levels of violence and brutality reached in the Syrian Civil War can be disheartening. There are however a lot of good people doing important work to help the people affected by the conflict. I've included links to a few of these organizations below.

If you can have only one thing, make it love.

-Abu Salaam

**American Refugee Committee:**

Arcrelief.org/donate

**International Rescue Committee:**

Rescue.org/donate

**Médecins Sans Frontières:**

msf.org/en/donate

**United Nations Children's Emergency Fund:**

support.unicef.org

Allahu Akbar - الله أكبر - God is Great!

Burqa - برقع - Publically worn women's outer garment

Captagon - Fenethylline - A psychostimulant with effects similar to a mixture and caffeine and amphetamine

Daesh - داعش - Islamic abbreviation for the Islamic State of Iraq and Syria - ad-Dawlah al-Islāmiyah fī 'l-ʿIrāq wa-sh-Shām

Dawlah - دولة - State

Hajj - حج - Pilgrimage

Halaal - حلال - Permissible/Allowed

(Al)Hamdulillah- الحمد لله - Praise God/Thank God

Haraam - حرام - Prohibited/Sinful

Hejira - هجرة - A Journey/ Honorably running away

Inshallah - إن شاء الله - God willing

Jihad - جهاد - Struggle

Kuffar - كفَّار - Disbelievers

Mashallah – ما شاء الله – God has willed it

Mufti - مفتي - Interpreter/expounder of Islamic law

Muharib - محارب - Warrior/Fighter (Plural: Muharibūn)

Mujahid - مجاهد - One who struggle in the name of Allah (Plural: Mujahideen)

Nasheeds - نشيد - A Cappella Islamic choral music

Sharia - شريعة - Islamic system of religous laws

Shukran - شكرا - Thanks

(As)Salaam Alaikum - سلام عليكم - Peace be upon you

Takbir - تَكْبِير - Exclamation of Allahu Akbar

Takfir - تكفير - One Muslim accusing another of apostasy

Walaikum Assalaam - وعليكم السلام - And upon you, peace

Made in the USA
Las Vegas, NV
29 December 2024